Nicholas Patrick Wiseman

Two Mysteries

Or Sacred Dramas for Convents or Families

Nicholas Patrick Wiseman

Two Mysteries
Or Sacred Dramas for Convents or Families

ISBN/EAN: 9783743427648

Manufactured in Europe, USA, Canada, Australia, Japa

Cover: Foto ©Andreas Hilbeck / pixelio.de

Manufactured and distributed by brebook publishing software
(www.brebook.com)

Nicholas Patrick Wiseman

Two Mysteries

TWO MYSTERIES:

OR SACRED DRAMAS FOR CONVENTS OR FAMILIES.

CHRISTMAS-NIGHT AND ST. URSULA.

GIVEN BY

H. E. CARD. WISEMAN,

ARCHBISHOP OF WESTMINSTER,

TO THE PROVIDENCE-ROW NIGHT REFUGE.

LONDON:

JOHN PHILP, 7, ORCHARD STREET,

PORTMAN SQUARE.

1863.

PREFACE.

THE firſt of theſe little pieces was compoſed for the Orphans of St. Margaret's Home, in Queen Square, and was acted by them at Chriſtmas, 1861. It has been repeated ſince in other places.

The ſecond was written at the requeſt of the children of St. Urſula's convent, at Upton, near Stratford ; who firſt exacted a promiſe of compliance with what they were going to aſk. Though the ſubject was not eaſy, a promiſe to children is too ſacred an engagement not to be fulfilled.

Both pieces having often been aſked for, it has been thought well to publiſh them, for a purpoſe which will ſecure indulgence to their defects.

THE SHEPHERDESSES AT
BETHLEHEM.

DIRECTIONS.

THE ſtage muſt be divided into two parts, by a curtain acroſs from ſide to ſide.

The front darkened repreſents the country, which may be done by evergreens or branches at the ſides; the piece begins here, and ſo proceeds to p. 19.

As there directed, the curtain which divides the ſtage is raiſed, and diſcovers the *tableau* of the Nativity, which ſhould be repreſented by real perſons, except the Infant. A gauze curtain or ſcreen ſhould be placed between the repreſentation and the audience (behind the inner curtain). The vignette is intended to aſſiſt in the preparation of this ſcene.

The Shepherdeſſes at Bethlehem.

ABIGAIL, RACHEL, REBECCA, Shepherdeſſes.

ABIGAIL *and* RACHEL *aſleep on either ſide.* *Muſic* (Gloria
in Excelſis).

ABIGAIL (*waking*).

WHAT ſweet muſic is this that I hear? Whence
does it come? It ſeems to be in the ſkies.
[*Looks around and above.*] There muſt be a
multitude of the heavenly hoſt joining in it!
Hark again! [*Muſic repeated.*] I am ſure none of our ſhepherds ever ſang like this. I will go and ſee. [*Starts up.*]
But where are they? There are their flocks, quietly lying and
ſleeping, with no one to guard them. I muſt find them;
ſomething ſingular muſt have happened, and I am ſure this
lovely muſic muſt have ſomething to do with it. [*Goes out.*

RACHEL (*ſpringing up*).

Have I been dreaming? What beautiful words I have heard in my ſleep—" Glory be to God on high, and peace on earth to men of good will,"—I am ſure thoſe were the words. I never heard them before—they do not belong to any of our ſongs—I do not recollect hearing them ſung in the ſynagogue or temple; though certainly it appeared to me as if they formed a delightful hymn. I am ſure none of our poor people could have imagined ſuch a ſublime thought, or put it into words; " Glory to God on high,"—what a beautiful expreſſion! why, it is juſt what heavenly ſpirits would ſing round His throne, ſeraphim and cherubim, beating their golden wings, as the prophets deſcribe them, and ever praiſing God! Ah! ſhall I too one day do this with them? " Peace," in the mean time, " peace on earth, to all who with good will ſeek it in a virtuous life." What conſolation I already find in theſe dear words! Every morning, on waking, I will repeat them. " Glory be to God," and " peace to men." [*Looks about.*] But what is become of my dear ſiſter? I ſaw her faſt aſleep near me before I laid down myſelf. Oh! I hope nothing has befallen her! [*Calls out.*] Abigail! Abigail! where are you? Oh, come here, and let me ſee you!—No one anſwers—ſurely ſome of the ſhepherds muſt have heard me. [*Looking.*] But they are gone too—and I am here all alone—what can have happened? Good God, protect me!   [*Weeps.*

ABIGAIL (*rushing in*).

My dear fifter, what has happened—why do you weep?

RACHEL (*embracing her*).

O my dear fifter, I was afraid fome accident had befallen you, as I did not fee you here. Oh, what fhould I do without you, if left alone! Poor helplefs orphans, as we are, we ftand in need of one another.

ABIGAIL.

And of God, now our only Father—but fuch a good one!

RACHEL.

Yes, indeed! for to Him we owe everything. What would have become of us, if He had not moved the heart of thofe good fhepherds to take us into their houfe, and take care of us, and bring us up in His fear. In their houfe we have indeed found true mothers, who treat us as they would their own children.

ABIGAIL.

But why were you fo alarmed about me, with fuch good friends near?

RACHEL.

It was becaufe I miffed, firft you, and afterwards them. Where were you all gone?

ABIGAIL.

Why, I went to feek *them*, and hoped to return before you awoke. You were faft afleep.

Rachel.

Afleep? But how impoffible it was to remain afleep, with fuch lovely dreams as I faw, or rather heard!

Abigail.

Then it could not be a dream, for it awoke me too; and I heard it when quite awake. Moft fweet mufic, was it not?

Rachel.

I dare fay—but I only noticed the words, they were fo beautiful.

Abigail.

And I was fo tranfported by the heavenly fong, that I have no idea of the words!

Rachel.

Wonderful! Then did you go to difcover whence it all came?

Abigail.

Yes, dear, and feeing all the fhepherds going towards the town, I ran after them, and only overtook the boy Samuel, who told me an angel had ordered them all to go to Bethlehem.

Rachel.

What for? They had only left it a few hours ago.

Abigail.

He faid the angel told them, that they would find there a child in a ftable; and that it was the Saviour of the world!

RACHEL.

Poor Samuel! He can have underſtood very little of the matter. It is not a very likely ſtory. But here comes our couſin Rebecca; and, if anything good is going on, ſhe is *ſure* to know it.

ABIGAIL.

Welcome, Rebecca, what brings you here?

Enter REBECCA.

REBECCA.

Good night, dear children; I have come out from Jeruſalem, to ſee with my own eyes if what I have heard is true.

ABIGAIL.

What is *that*, dear?

REBECCA.

Tell me firſt, have you ſeen anything?

ABIGAIL.

No; but I have heard the moſt beautiful muſic.

REBECCA.

Perhaps it was a dream?

ABIGAIL.

No; for I heard it diſtinctly after I was awake.

REBECCA.

And you, Rachel?

RACHEL.

I heard it, too; but attended more to the words.

REBECCA.

What were they?

RACHEL.

" Glory be to God on high, and peace on earth to men of good will."

REBECCA.

Ah, how beautiful! They found exactly right.

RACHEL.

Right for what?

REBECCA.

For the birth of that Child in Bethlehem.

ABIGAIL.

Then there *is* a child born there? Samuel was correct.

REBECCA.

Explain yourfelf, dear; what could Samuel know about it?

ABIGAIL.

I ran after the fhepherds, who were all going to Bethlehem; and Samuel, whom I overtook, told me, an angel had ordered them to go there, and find a child in a ftable, who fhould be the Saviour of the world! It feems very ftrange!

REBECCA (*raiſing her hands and eyes to Heaven*).

Praiſe be to God! It is all true! Oh, come, let us go to the City of David, and bid his Son, our King, welcome to earth.

RACHEL.

How do you mean? What have poor ſhepherdeſſes like us to do with kings, or royal infants?

REBECCA.

Liſten to me, children, and I will tell you all. Yeſterday, when in Jeruſalem, I ſaw that holy old man, Simeon, coming as uſual out of the Temple, with a crowd round him, aſking his prayers and bleſſing. Always before, I had ſeen him bent down, with his long white beard reſting on his breaſt; but now he walked erect, and his countenance, uſually melancholy, was quite radiant, and tears of joy filled his eyes, as he kept exclaiming: " He comes, He comes, this very night." Some people ſaid the venerable old man was going out of his mind. All were amazed. I went up to him, and kiſſed his hand; and as I looked up into his beautiful face, he looked down at me, moſt kindly, and ſaid: " Are you not from Bethlehem?" I ſaid I was; a poor peaſant. " Then go, my child," he re-plied, " haſte, loſe no time, be there to-night, and ſee Him, juſt born." " Whom?" I aſked. " The Saviour of the world, the King of Iſrael," he ſaid. Then I exclaimed, as you did: " How can I pretend to enter into the palace of a king?

How fhall I get through his guards and courtiers?" He fhed tears, as he anfwered me: " Palace, child? Alas! a ftable. His only guard is the good fimple carpenter, Jofeph. His only attendant is the fweeteft of mothers, Mary, the child of my former dear friend Joachim, pure as a lily, beautiful as a rofe, bright as a ftar, and perfect as an angel! She will let you fondle, and carefs, and embrace her darling babe.

" Run, my daughter. I fhall fee Him in a few days, then die in peace. You fee Him before me. Firft the angels are to fee Him alone with Mary and Jofeph; next come the fhepherds, for He is the Good Shepherd. An angel to-night will invite them."

ABIGAIL *and* RACHEL.

It is true, then, all true!

REBECCA.

As I was haftening away, I met the holy widow and pro-phetefs, Anna, who confirmed all to me. Come, then, let us, too, haften to Bethlehem, and adore this heavenly Child.

ABIGAIL.

Come, let us go, and leave our flocks to the care of holy angels.

RACHEL.

Wolves themfelves muft be hufhed and tamed this happy night.

[*They retire, two to one fide, the third to the other. The* ADESTE FIDELES *is fung. At the verfe* NATUM VIDETE *the curtain draws up, and the Tableau of the Nativity appears. They fall on their knees till the end of the verfe. Then they rife, and go on.*

ABIGAIL.

Angels bright! is this the place,
Where we fhould feek this Child of grace?
For a palace, in a ftable,
With the manger for His bed!
Was not man to furnifh able
A better roof above His head,
Or a fofter couch to fpread?
Angels fair! your wings unfold,
To fcreen from winter's nipping cold,
That tender flefh, thofe trembling limbs!
And lull, with your moft foothing hymns,
That darling Babe to gentle fleep.

RACHEL.

See, dear fifter, fee Him weep!
Lovely Infant! for what reafon?
'Tis not the inclement feafon—
'Tis not that Thy fweet eyes borrow,
From dear Mary's, looks of forrow—

For her face is flufhed with joy,
Gazing on her peerlefs boy.
No, the fountain's not on earth
Where thofe ftreams receive their birth ;
Whofe each brilliant drop appears
Bright as gems the High Prieft wears.

Rebecca.

True, dear friends, for yefterday,
I heard the good old Anna fay,
The Child in Bethlehem to be born,
So beautiful, yet fo forlorn,
Was deftined, after grief and lofs—
After buffets, ftripes, and fcorn—
To die upon a fhameful Crofs !

Abigail.

Oh, no, no ! it cannot be
For one fo good, fo fweet as He !

Rachel.

At leaft as yet He cannot know
This dreadful fate.

Rebecca.

Alas, not fo !
This Child is God, Who all created,
Who knoweth all above, below.

ABIGAIL *and* RACHEL.

God! How thus can *He* be treated!

REBECCA.

Ah, dear children! for our fins—
Yours and mine—He now begins
A life of forrows, to be ended
Only when, with arms extended,
On the Crofs He yields His breath,
To buy us life with His own death.

ABIGAIL.

Oh! dear Infant, can I ever
Be to Thee a caufe of pain?

RACHEL.

Bleffed Child! Oh, I will never
Sin, and bring thee grief again!

BOTH (*kneeling*).

With our heart and foul we love Thee!
With Thee, her who bends above Thee!
We are children, Thou our Brother,
We are orphans, fhe our mother.
Make us be like both of you,
Pious, meek, obedient, true,
Faithful, humble, and refigned,

Loving God and all mankind.
If we love Thy Chriſtmas tree,
May we love Thy Croſs no leſs,
Each our joys or griefs will bleſs—
Where'er *Thou* art, Thine orphans wiſh to be!

[*The Curtain drops.*

ST. URSULA.

WRITTEN FOR THE CHILDREN OF ST. URSULA'S
CONVENT, UPTON.

DRAMATIS PERSONÆ.

URSULA.

BERTHA. ETHELDREDA.

WARBURGA. MARGARET.

Scene, *Cologne.*

Prologue to the Myſtery of
St. Urſula.

SPOKEN BY ONE OF ST. URSULA'S CHILDREN.

AY, in this world, ſo dreary, dark, and chill,
What is the balm which cures each chiefeſt ill;
What is the light our infant ſteps which cheers,
Which guides our youth, and ſoothes our
      waning years;
Which death forgets to quench, and ſin to ſpoil,
Our reſt in trouble, and our ſtay in toil;
A joy of earth, yet borrowed from above;
What is this? ſay—It is a Mother's love.
  O boon beneficent; O love moſt pure!
Strong 'mid the feeble, 'mid the fleeting ſure;
A flower of Eden ſnatched from Satan's ſnare;
A prize the ſpoiler's hand is forced to ſpare;

'Mid fcenes of vengeance, ftamped with Heaven's own mark,*
And borne on furging waves fafe in the buoyant ark.†
    What marvel ? fince in Jefus' facred heart
A mother's love was deftined to have part ;
With fweet attraction mutual to entwine
The finlefs Mother and the Son Divine ;
And e'en on Calvary our Lord would prove
How dear to God is holy mother-love :
When to His friend he gave that Mother lone
That fhe might be his charge, his gueft, his own.‡
    Children of Mary bleft ! to me, to you,
This love is ever conftant, ever new ;
Unchanged by time, unlimited by place,
Since built on promife and fecured by grace ;
Nor diftance chills it, nor caprice impairs,
Each child of Mary all her beauty fhares ;
She to her foft'ring love the orphan takes
Whom father fpurns, and mother e'en forfakes ;
Earth's little ones may lack their rightful food,
But Mary's children know no orphanhood.
    Children of Urfula ! ye, too, full well
The folace of maternal love could tell ;

---

* Alluding to the prefervation of the firftborn of Ifrael.
† Genefis vi. 18.   ‡ See St. John, xix. 27. " in fua."

What though your Mother, throned in blifs on high,
Watch not your toils and pains with flefhly eye;
Yet e'en on earth, in fweet Religion's fchool,
She lives, in folemn rite and holy rule,
A conftant, deathlefs life which ne'er fhall end,
Till to her throne your gladfome fteps ye bend.
What though fhe mifs, in Anglia's peaceful clime,
The fterner features of her Order's prime;
And trace the marks of Chrift's moft holy Rood
In lines of penance, not in print of blood;
Yet, as the eagle, from her eyrie's height,
Spurns not the brood which tracks unmoved the light;
So fhe the child will own, whofe earneft eye
Fronts with unfwerving gaze the Light on high.

Still, as the fervour of our faith grows cold,
We fearch the annals of our Saints of old,
And ftore the lamps, whofe food hath run its courfe,
With oil frefh welling from the fountain's fource.

E'en fuch a ftory of the earlier days
We re-enact to-night, and afk, not praife,
But kind indulgence, while in fimple verfe,
A tale of faintly moral we rehearfe,
How in Colonia once, a faithful band
Of Virgin martyrs purpled Rhenus' ftrand

With blood which glow'd, and glows, in Englifh veins,
Through Upton's valleys, or on Effex' plains ;
Prompt to defend, at Jefus' loving call,
His glorious Crofs—our joy, our hope, our all.

F. O.

In the following piece, advantage has been taken of recent refearches into the hiftory of St. Urfula, which, among other interefting difcoveries, feem to eftablifh the fact of her martyrdom being due to the Vandals, returning home after a great defeat in Gaul.—See the laft volume of the *Bollandifts.*

St. Urfula, and her young virgin companions, are fuppofed to be paffing through Cologne, in pilgrimage to Rome.

St. Urfula.

SCENE I.

URSULA *with* BERTHA *and* ETHELDREDA, *one on each fide.*

URSULA.

FEAR, my daughters, that the news are true.
The heathen Vandals with increafing rage
Are haftening to their native faftneffes,
Revenging, as they march, their late defeat.
They pillage nought, but all deftroy.   No church
Or holy fhrine is facred in their eyes;
But, like a legion of unbridled demons,
They ply the burning brand on every fide,
Until it flafhes up to heaven in flame,
Then falls to earth in afhes.

BERTHA.
                         Does their fury
Thus wreak itfelf on things unfeeling only?
If fo, 'tis well.   Walls may be built again.

ETHELDREDA.

I fear not, fifter, for I heard it faid
That they have maffacred unfparingly,
Man, woman, child, e'en God's own minifters.

URSULA.

It is too true indeed : the *torch* they bear
In their *left* hand ; their *fwords* are in their *right*,
As red with gore, as that with lurid fire.

BERTHA.

But in Cologne, at leaft, we're fafe ; its walls
Are ftrong, and ftudded with high baftion-towers.
On thofe ftand clad in mail, bright-crefted knights ;
While upon thefe, with quick unerring aim,
Arrayed are ftalwart bowmen.   Surely here
The torrent of barbarian violence
Will be rolled back upon itfelf, and turned
Into another channel.

URSULA.

           'Twill be fo,
If it pleafe God.   But if in His great wrath,
To punifh fin, or in His gracious love,
To crown His Church with martyrdom's frefh wreaths,
He grants thefe infidels a paffing power,
Nor walls, nor towers, nor knights will aught avail.

ETHELDREDA.

'Twill be, methinks, like what a pilgrim told me,
Happens, not feldom, on Campania's fhore,
In happy Italy.   From dark Vefuvius
Rolls down a burning ftream, wave upon wave,
With flow, but fure, deftruction in its bed,
Covering vineyards, gardens, faireft crops,
With blackeft defolation.   If it meet
A rock or wall, this feems to ftay its courfe,
Till billow piled on billow reach its fummit,
Then the next pours itfelf over the brim.
So may it be with thefe barbarians.

BERTHA (*who has fhown great terror during this fpeech*).

Then let us fly at once, dear Urfula !

URSULA.

My child, it is too late : the town's beleaguered.

ETHELDREDA.

Early this morning, from my lofty chamber,
I faw the Vandal camp, with banners flying,
All round the walls.

BERTHA.

Then hafte !   Oh, let us fly,
Down the fwift Rhine, whofe ftream will bear us
    quick
Towards our own Englifh home.

ETHELDREDA.

The favages have drawn acrofs the ftream
A chain, which will arreft the ftrongeft bark ;
With guards at either end.

BERTHA.

O heavens! Is no hope, then, left of fafety ?
No hiding-place, no way, or means of flight ?
Why did I leave my father's houfe fo calm,
My mother's fond embrace, my fifters' fmiles,
Here to be butchered in a foreign land ?

URSULA (*careffing her*).

Say rather martyred, if God give you grace.

BERTHA.

O Urfula, our mother now, protect me ;
I am too young to die.

URSULA.

         For fhame, dear Bertha!
Think of the babes that Herod's foldiers tore,
Sucklings as yet, from their poor mothers' bofoms,
And flaughtered cruelly. They were young, indeed!

BERTHA.

Ay, young and innocent! [*Weeps.*] But what am I ?
Their very title marks our difference.

ETHELDREDA.

Brought up from infancy by pious parents,
Then from youth's growing dangers fafely guarded,
In cloiftered walls; unftained by fin or malice,
Yours is a virtuous life.

BERTHA.

Dear Etheldreda!
Yours has been always fuch. You know how often
You ufed to chide me for my giddy ways,
My love of ornament and foolifh toys;
For though your looks were gentle, fweet your words,
Your ftern example was your fureft arm.
Bertha a martyr! 'twould difgrace the name;
A thoughtlefs fchoolgirl to be called a faint!

ETHELDREDA.

Why not? who makes the call will give the grace.
I own I feel a glowing in my breaft
Of a new warmth—an ardour it doth feem,
To grafp the palm-branch that hangs clofe above me.

URSULA.

Beware, dear Etheldreda, O beware!
There is more danger in this eagernefs
Than in poor Bertha's cowardice. Of old

Many a crown, we read, has been withdrawn
From over-boldnefs—

ETHELDREDA (*abforbed*).
         Pardon me, dear mother !
         [*Taking Urfula's hand and kiffing it.*
You are too gentle, it is proud prefumption,
Enough to rob me of what I pretend to.

URSULA.
No, deareft child, no more are you prefumptuous,
Than Bertha is a coward, as I called her,
I afk forgivenefs of you both, fweet friends.

BERTHA.
O no, you fpoke but truth.   Have patience with me,
If I lay bare the weaknefs of my foul.
I do remember me thofe happy days,
I paffed near Epping's foreft, there we roamed
Through tangled paths, and watched, in leafy glades,
The graceful ftag, toffing his noble antlers,
Heard the quaint chatter of the painted jay,
Or plucked the wild flowers for Our Lady's wreath.
Sometimes I think of our calm home at Upton,
How there, between the hours of tafk and prayer,
On the green fward beneath our fpreading cedar,
We frifked like lambs, finlefs and free as they.

This is the world to which I feel attached,
Not to the baubles, vanities, and cares
Of that whereof we knew not.

ETHÈLDREDA.

                  Happy Bertha!
How far more worthy of a crown than I!
Your facrifice is far more meritorious,
For it confifts in what might well be loved ;
Your victim is the lamb you have defcribed,
Yourfelf—but fee Warburga is approaching,
She feems as ever quite abforbed in prayer.

SCENE II.

Enter WARBURGA, *as if feeing no one, with her eyes on the
ground, and her hands clafped. The others give way and
fhe ftands forward in the middle.*

WARBURGA.

AN it be true? had I juft reached the goal
So often prayed for fince my infancy ?
E'en at my mother's knee I ufed to think
How bleffed it muft be to die for Chrift ;
Doubly a victim—dead to felf and earth !

Daily I pray'd for this all-paſſing grace,
Of which I knew myſelf unworthy.   Yet
My prayer ſeemed to be heard—my Spouſe's cup
Had well-nigh reached my lips, this very morn,
To drink of it with Him, when lo! 'tis daſhed
Down, in one moment, to the very ground!
Becauſe one of our Engliſh virgin-band
Hath ſhown ſome imperfection.   Well I know
It muſt be I! the others are ſo holy,
And I'm ſo poor in virtue, that none elſe
Can ſtand between them and their crown.   Indeed
This muſt not be; but I muſt ſacrifice
My long and earneſt wiſhes, for their ſakes.

    [*Kneels, with arms croſſed, and looking up to Heaven.*

Father and Lord!   Thou knoweſt, from my childhood,
How I have envied holy Agnes, young,
And yet a martyr!   I have longed and prayed,
With burning thirſt of love, to be with her,
For that is being with my Spouſe and Mother.
I have juſt reached her age, and it hath ſeemed
As if hope dawned on me, of further likeneſs,
But no; I am unworthy of this grace.

    [*Hangs down her head between her hands and weeps.*

Inſtead then of the holocauſt of life,

Accept the facrifice of thefe defires.

If my unworthinefs the hindrance makes,

That keeps my darling fifters from their prize,

Spare *me* alone e'en to decrepit age,

To fpin and toil in fervice of Thy poor:

Till, through the prayers of thefe Thy youthful martyrs,

I may find place to fit beneath their feet,

And " venerate the palms "* I may not fhare.

> [*With hands ftretched towards the ground.*

Here at Thy footftool I lay my poor offering,

Surrendering to Thee my heart's fole longing,

From childhood till this hour; quench not its flame,

Even though ufelefs now; 'twill give ftill light,

If no more warmth, to my cold lonely faith!

> [BERTHA *rufhes forward and feizes her arm; fhe*
> *ftands up confufed.*

BERTHA.

Stop, fifter, ftay, fpeak not fuch cruel words;

Have you not heard it?

WARBURGA.

> No (*penfively*). It *muft* be I.

ETHELDREDA.

To what did you allude? Ah! yes, I know,

* Collect of St. Urfula.

You have been favoured with fome bleffed vifion,
And there have heard of my prefumption,
My name being kindly fpared—

WARBURGA.

                              A vifion?
How can *I* have fuch gifts?—They are for faints.

ETHELDREDA.

Then call it what you will; but tell us, deareft,
What you have feen or heard.

WARBURGA.

                    The truth is, fifter,
I am fo lazy, or diftracted oft
In prayer, that I do fear I fall afleep,
And dream ftrange dreams. This morning, ay, juft now,
Looking towards Heaven with its lovely fky,
This muft have happened; for I faw a fight
Glorious and beautiful, but yet it faddened me.

URSULA.

Tell us, dear daughter, all you faw or dreamt.

WARBURGA.

Methought I faw againft the azure fky
A moft brave knight, arrayed in golden panoply,
With fhield that looked like one huge diamond knot,

Dafhing out fparks whitherfoe'er it turned:
So that, if towards the Vandal camp it looked,
Men dropped their weapons, fheltering their eyes.
Upon a milk-white charger, filver harneffed,
Mounted, he feemed to trample down the clouds.

URSULA.

It was St. George of England.

WARBURGA.

Yes! 'twas he;
Oft have I feen him, on our way, efcorting us,
With troops of joyous angels—all our guardians—
Holding him confort; *now* he was alone,
And feemed as forrowful as faints may look.

ETHELDREDA.

Oh, what an awful caufe muft there have been!

WARBURGA.

I feared it was in me!

BERTHA.

No! in me rather.
O fifter dear, proceed.

WARBURGA.

I, too, began
To grieve me much; when fuddenly the found

Of notes angelic fwelled upon the breeze,
Firft in the far horizon. When I looked,
I faw what feemed a cloud of fummer midges;
But quick they grew, upon my eye and ear,
To angels' likenefs, and to angels' ftrain.
Yet it did feem as if a waving wood
Were flying with them through the air; for each
Carried a palm-branch, green as if frefh-plucked.
So armed, they haftened to the champion-faint
And greeted him in loving cadences,
Fluttering round him on their golden wings.
Then he with eyes averted afked, " Whence come ye ?"

ETHELDREDA.

What did they anfwer?

WARBURGA.

           One fpoke for the hoft,
A prince amidft the reft, though princes all—
England's own guardian. Thus he warbled forth,
In fuch fweet tone and accent, that the nightingale
Might well have died of envy, had he heard them.

I.

We have failed along Egypt's bleak fhore,
  We have flitted o'er Araby's wafte,

We have fkimmed the grey walls of Tadmor,*
And we've come back, thus laden, in hafte.

II.

For we gathered our palms as we went,
    And we trimmed them while hitherward flying,
One, with each Virgin's lily-ftalk blent,
    We will place in her hand at her dying.

III.

And fo now round the city we hover,
    Ready foon as each Martyr fhall fall,
With our wings her pure relics to cover,
    Not lefs bright fhould be martyrdom's pall.

ETHELDREDA.

How fweet a ftrain! I would I could have heard it!

URSULA.

And what did then the holy knight reply?

WARBURGA (*forrowful and hefitating*).

" Caft down," he faid, " Angels, your needlefs burthen.
One of your charge hath wavered, and fears death;
So I muft fave her; and for her fave all.
I'll turn my fhield on the barbarian foe,
And ftrike a panic in them, fo they'll fly.

* Palmyra, the city of palms.

For 'twould bring fhame upon the Englifh name,
If only one among our noble damfels
Quailed before death for Chrift."
                              So fearing left
Some weaknefs in my heart, to the keen eye
Of Saints apparent, might be lurking from me,
The fraileft and the leaft, I came down to you,
Dear mother Urfula, for confolation.

    BERTHA (*who has been much afflicted, coming forward*).
No, I repeat I am the culprit.   Oh!
How dreadful now appears to me my guilt,
I may have robbed you all of inftant glory,
And that the brighteft, moft fublime in heaven!
Is it too late, dear mother, to retrieve
My folly and ingratitude?   Oh! let me go,—
Warburga, take me—to the altar's foot,
And witnefs thence to all thofe holy Spirits
My deep repentance, and I hope forgivenefs.
It may not be too late, the palms as yet
May not have dropped from their angelic hands:—
Or mine alone; I'll be content to bear it
Soiled with earth's clay, as it muft needs be now.
                   URSULA.
Take her, good child, to give her forrows vent,
For a mere childifh weaknefs that is paft.

[WARBURGA *takes* BERTHA *by the hand and is leading her out, when* ETHELDREDA *takes* WARBURGA'S *other hand.*

ETHELDREDA.

Let me go with you, for I have been proud,
And have defpifed my fifter's timidnefs.

[*Exeunt* WARBURGA, BERTHA, *and* ETHELDREDA.

SCENE III.

URSULA (*alone*).

OW difficult it is to keep the path,
Which, without fwerving to the right or left,
Leads ftraight to God! One only can it be.
If from this earth we had to reach the fun,
The fureft, fhorteft way would be to climb
The beam that comes direct from him to us.
So to the Centre of immortal light
The trueft path muft be His brighteft ray—
The emanation of His mighty Will.
If upon this I ftand, on this I move,
I cannot err, it binds me faft to Him,
And to Him draws me ftraight.
                    What matters it,

If I this day a Martyr die, or live?
Whiche'er He willeth, that is beſt for me.
I am unworthy of ſo high a grace,
Yet may I not refuſe it freely given.
My own unworthineſs, and God's great love,
Thus balance one another in my ſoul.
Like wings outſtretched, they poiſe my doubtful thoughts,
And keep them on that ſtraight, unfailing track.
  Should that ſublimer deſtiny await me,
I aſk not that my aſhes, or my ſiſters',
Should be enſhrined in ſome majeſtic church,
Colonia's pride ; but rather that our memory
May be ſuggeſtive of a great deſign
To ſome angelic mind,* for reſcuing
From the world's ſnares, and training up for God
Maidens and children, ſuch as follow me
To Rome or heaven, as beſt pleaſes God.
But here return my children.

                    * St. Angela Merici, foundreſs of the Urſulines.

SCENE IV.

Enter WARBURGA, BERTHA, *and* ETHELDREDA. URSULA
takes BERTHA *by the hand.*

URSULA.

ARLING Bertha,
How bright you look! I know I need not afk
The reafon of this change. God blefs you.

[*Embraces her.*

ETHELDREDA.

Oh! had you feen her, deareft mother, when
Wilfrid our venerable chaplain led her
Before the altar to make her oblation;
So calm, fo radiant, you would have faid,
It was an angel child come down to lead us.

WARBURGA.

So delicately humble was her fpeech,
And yet fo refolute, it muft have won,
If I have loft, the grace we all defire.

BERTHA.

Oh! fpoil not by your undeferved praife
The willing reparation of my fault.

Would it had been more perfect.   But, dear mother,
One act is wanting to complete it.

URSULA.

What ?

BERTHA.

That you ſhould ratify my offering.
Let it paſs through your hands, or rather, rather—

[*Heſitating and baſhful.*

URSULA.

Speak, deareſt child.

BERTHA (*kneeling at her right*).

Oh ! let me be your Iſaac,

And you my Abraham ; ſlay me with your will,
Offer me whole-burnt in my heart's own flame,
A victim to Chriſt's love ; but let no lamb
Come between me and perfect immolation.
Give me to God for death, as you have given me
For life thus far !

    [URSULA, *deeply moved, places her right hand on her head,*
       extending the left, and looking up to Heaven.   The other
       two look on in attitudes of reverence and tenderneſs.

URSULA *ſpeaks with great ſolemnity.*

I.

O great God, our Creator,
    Through Whom we all live,

To Whom, early or later,
 Life back we muſt give.

II.

O good God, our Redeemer,
 By Whom we were ſaved,
When firſt martyrdom's ſtreamer
 On Golgotha waved.

III.

O ſweet God, our Conſoler,
 In Whom is all love,
Light more bright·than the ſolar,
 Though placed far above.

IV.

(To us, life is ſalvation,
 Salvation is love ;)
Accept now the oblation
 Of this trembling dove.

V.

God, great, merciful, gracious !
 Tranſplant this ſweet flower,
With its fragrance ſo precious,
 To Mary's bright bower.

      [*A diſtant tumult is heard, ſhouts,*
       (*and trumpets, if poſſible*).

SCENE V.

Enter MARGARET, *rushing in.*

MARGARET.

HOW glad I am to find you, sweetest mother,
And dear companions.   All is over now,
As far as earth goes.

URSULA.

                        Tell me, my good child,
What meant that shout, what are the news you bear?

MARGARET.

From a high casement I have watched the town,
Save during hours of more important duties.
At early dawn began the fierce attack
Upon the city walls; some of the foe
Rushed to the breaches in the battered walls;
Some bearing ladders tried to scale what stood.
Hour after hour, though gallantly repulsed,
They came in countless hordes, with savage cries,
Fresh from the camp, upon our wearied knights.
Terrible was the crash each time they met,
Till well-nigh the huge heaps of hideous corpses,

Not only filled the moat, but fpared the ufe
Of ladders to the fell barbarians.

ETHELDREDA.

O Margaret, how could you gaze fo long
On fuch a cruel fight?

MARGARET.

Yet feemed it not fuch.

For in the very midft of the wall's ruins,
Towering above all, ours and our enemies,
Stood noble Geryon, my brother's friend ;
His burnifhed cuirafs, and his waving plume,
Made him confpicuous amid the medley.
How he encouraged Chriftians by his words,
How he drove back the Paynims with his fword
Would be for knights to tell.

An hour ago
Methought the chance of battle was with ours.

BERTHA.

An hour ago?

MARGARET.

I think it muft be fo.

ETHELDREDA.

What happened then?

MARGARET.

The heathens dropped their arms,

Retreated, fhading with their hands their eyes,
As though a fudden burft of light had dazzled them.

          WARBURGA.

And what did ours?

          MARGARET.

                    Purfued them for a fpace,
Geryon in the van.

          URSULA (*addreffing* WARBURGA).

                    This was the time
Our champion faint gazed on them through his fhield.
How long did this advantage laft?

          MARGARET.

Not many minutes; foon the foemen rallied
With unrelenting fury, when, alas!
Came the calamity of this fad day!

          BERTHA.

What do you mean?

          MARGARET.

                    The gallant Geryon
Pierced with innumerable wounds, fell flain,
A martyr to be honoured on our altars.

          ETHELDREDA.

What happened next?

          MARGARET.

                    Over the walls and towers,
As though they were a field-fence, leapt the foe,

And, flaughtering their defenders, through the ftreets
Ran headlong, fparing neither fex nor age.
Such of our fifters as lived near the walls
Are now with God above!

URSULA.

O pray for us,
Ye holy fouls, that we may come to you.

> [*Alarms, nearer.*

WARBURGA.

O bleffed fummons to our happy fate,
The enemy draws near, our prayers are heard!
But hark! heard you that ftrain of heavenly mufic?

> [*Mufic of harps, or other inftruments.*

URSULA.

Liften, above the tumult ftill it furges.

> [*They liften, then group themfelves round* URSULA,
> *who holds her long and ample mantle over them,*
> *kneeling two at each fide under it, as reprefented*
> *in the vignette. They fing alternately with the*
> *Angels.*

CHORUS OF ANGELS.

Maidens of Britain! the Lamb's holy brides,
Hafte to the banquet, He loving provides,
Come! come! come!

Chorus of Virgins.

Heavenly fpirits, our guardians on high,
Gladly, with you, to our Bridegroom we fly ;
  We come ! we come ! we come !

Angels.

Soiled are your garments yet ; firft wafh them white,
In the fount, from His Heart, gufhing fo bright ;
  Come ! come ! come !

Virgins.

Firft may they be in the crimfon flood dyed,
Rufhing foon in our own hearts' ebbing tide,
  We come ! we come ! we come !

Angels and Virgins.

This day of gladnefs, of glory, of grace,
Gives back to Virgins, with Martyrs, their place.

Angels.

Come ! come ! come !

Virgins.

  We come ! we come ! we come !

[During this laft chorus, the curtain defcends flowly.
 When it has dropped, a crafh of breaking in,
 fhouts and tumult.

CHISWICK PRESS :—PRINTED BY WHITTINGHAM AND WILKINS,
TOOKS COURT, CHANCERY LANE.

𝔐usic

FOR THE

Myſtery of S. Ursula.

The WORDS by His Eminence

Cardinal WISEMAN.

The MUSIC by the

Very Rev. E. Canon CROOKALL, D.D.

LONDON:

JOHN PHILP, 7, Orchard Street, Portman Square. W.

Music for the Mystery of S. Ursula.

I.—SONG OF ANGELS.

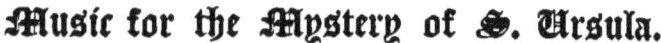

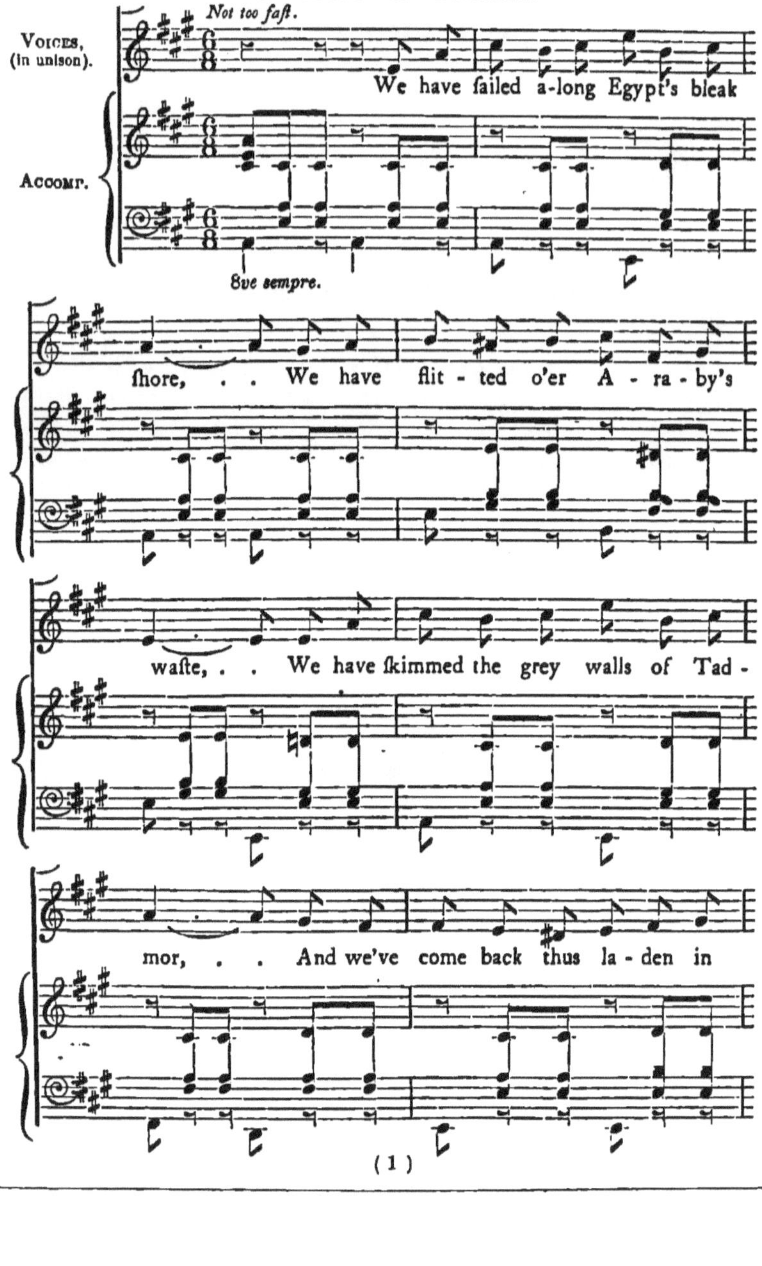
Not too fast.
Voices, (in unison).
Accomp.
We have sailed a-long Egypt's bleak
8ve sempre.
shore, . . We have flit - ted o'er A - ra - by's
waste, . . We have skimmed the grey walls of Tad -
mor, . . And we've come back thus la - den in

haste, in haste, And we've come back thus la-den in

haste. . . For we gath-ered our palms as we

went, . . And we trimmed them while hith-er-ward

fly-ing, One with each vir-gin's li-ly-stalk

(2)

blent, .. We will place in her hand at her

dy-ing,   One with each Vir-gin's li-ly ftalk

blent, .. We will place in her hand at her

dy - ing. And fo now round the ci - ty we

(3)

ho-ver, Rea - dy foon as each Mar - tyr fhall

fall, With our wings her pure re-lics to co-ver. Not lefs

bright fhould be mar - tyr-dom's pall, Not lefs bright, not lefs

bright fhould be mar - tyr - dom's pall. . .

II.—CHORUS OF ANGELS.

Spi - - rits our guard - ians on high, . .

Glad - ly with you . . to our Bridegroom, our Bridegroom we

fly. We come, we come, we come, we come, we come, we

come, we come, we come... Soiled are your garments yet,

(6)

first wash them white In the fount from His heart gush-ing so bright.

Come, come, come, come. First may they be in the

crimson flood dyed, Rushing soon in our heart's fast-ebb-ing tide. We

come, we come, we come, we come. This . . . day of

(7)

glad - - nefs, of glo - - ry and grace.

VIRGINS.

This . . day of

Gives . . back to

glad - - nefs, of glo - - ry and grace,

Gives back to

Vir - gins with martyrs, with mar-tyrs their place.

Gives back to

(8)

(9)

glo - - ry and grace, . . Gives . . back to

Vir - gins with martyrs, with mar-tyrs their place. Come,

ANGELS.

VIRGINS.

place.

come,

come, come, come,

We come, we come, we come, we

(11)